NIGHTTIME SYMPHONY

ATHENEUM BOOKS FOR YOUNG READERS ⸏ An imprint of Simon & Schuster Children's Publishing Division ⸏ 1230 Avenue of the Americas, New York, New York 10020
Text copyright © 2019 by Mosley Media, LLC and Christopher Myers ⸏ Illustrations copyright © 2019 by Christopher Myers and Kaa Illustration
All rights reserved, including the right of reproduction in whole or in part in any form. ⸏ ATHENEUM BOOKS FOR YOUNG READERS is a registered trademark of Simon & Schuster, Inc.
Atheneum logo is a trademark of Simon & Schuster, Inc. ⸏ For information about special discounts for bulk purchases, please contact Simon & Schuster Special Sales
at 1-866-506-1949 or business@simonandschuster.com.
The Simon & Schuster Speakers Bureau can bring authors to your live event. For more information or to book an event, contact the
Simon & Schuster Speakers Bureau at 1-866-248-3049 or visit our website at www.simonspeakers.com.
Jacket design by Ann Bobco and Semadar Megged; interior design by Semadar Megged ⸏ The text for this book was set in Kosmik. ⸏ The illustrations for this book were digitally rendered.
Manufactured in China ⸏ 0219 SCP ⸏ First Edition ⸏ 10 9 8 7 6 5 4 3 2 1
CIP data for this book is available from the Library of Congress.
ISBN 978-1-4424-1208-8
ISBN 978-1-4424-5438-5 (eBook)

TIMBALAND Feat. Christopher Myers

NIGHTTIME
SYMPHONY

Art by **Christopher Myers** and **Kaa Illustration**

Atheneum Books for Young Readers
New York London Toronto
Sydney New Delhi

hey there, darling baby child,
you're safe in here
though the storm is wild.

the streetlights glow
    through dark so deep

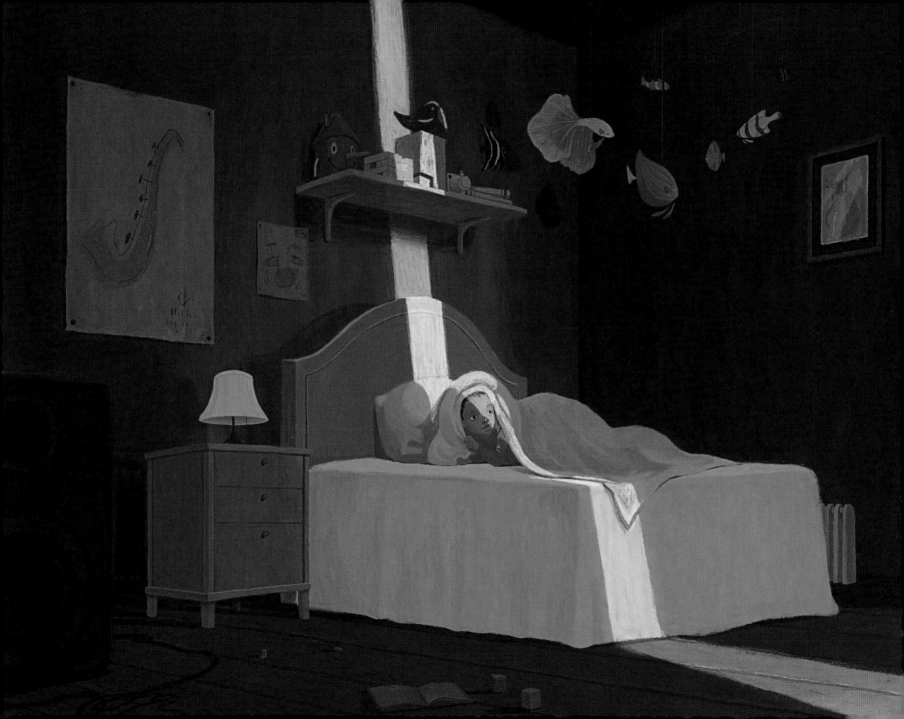

but safe in sound
    you'll go to sleep.

do you hear the raindrops tap
upon the windows of your nap?
the clouds pour down a steady beat
to soothe your slumber beneath the sheet.

the cars outside on
        streets so wet
    their headlights cast
a silhouette

of trees waving arms up in the air,
they dance for us like they don't care.

radios sing in every home,
    steady like the city's metronome.
        the bass is a pillow, soft and warm,
the whole world's tuned to the quiet storm.

is that lightning across the sky?
thunder soon comes
crashing by.
don't you worry, little one,
the angels too
are musicians.

hear the gutters rush like rivers?
don't cry or worry, shake or shiver.
no flood will pour in the place we stay—
that's just the music water plays.

the wind it howls,

it blows,

it sings—

nature's voice:

melody

and strings.

don't fear the raging storm so strong—

we'll remix the raging into a song.

last looks from nighttime
    windows high,
        an umbrella sea of passersby
with each turntable above each head—
    you're the dj to spin
        your sweet self to bed.

rain clouds blanket the whole wide world.
    inside the sounds of the storm you curl
like a crescent moon of rest—
    the tempest soon becomes your nest.

when the morning
comes around,
you'll remember
every sound.
sun breaks through the cloudy sky . . .

the storm was just a lullaby.